Published in 2018 by **Windmill Books**,
an Imprint of Rosen Publishing
29 East 21st Street, New York, NY 10010

Copyright © 2018 Blake Publishing

Cover and text design: Leanne Nobilio
Editor: Vanessa Barker

Photography: All images © Dreamstime.
Inside back cover illustration by Kim Webber.

Cataloging-in-Publication Data
Names: Johnson, Rebecca.
Title: Crafty crocodiles / Rebecca Johnson.
Description: New York : Windmill Books, 2018. | Series: Reptile
  adventures | Includes index.
Identifiers: ISBN 9781508193647 (pbk.) | ISBN 9781508193609
  (library bound) | ISBN 9781508193685 (6 pack)
Subjects: LCSH: Crocodiles–Juvenile literature.
Classification: LCC QL666.C925 J65 2018 | DDC 597.98'2–dc23

Manufactured in China
CPSIA Compliance Information: Batch BW18WM: For Further Information
contact Rosen Publishing, New York, New York at 1-800-237-9932

REPTILE ADVENTURES

CONTENTS

Come a little closer,
I'm Crafty Crocodile.

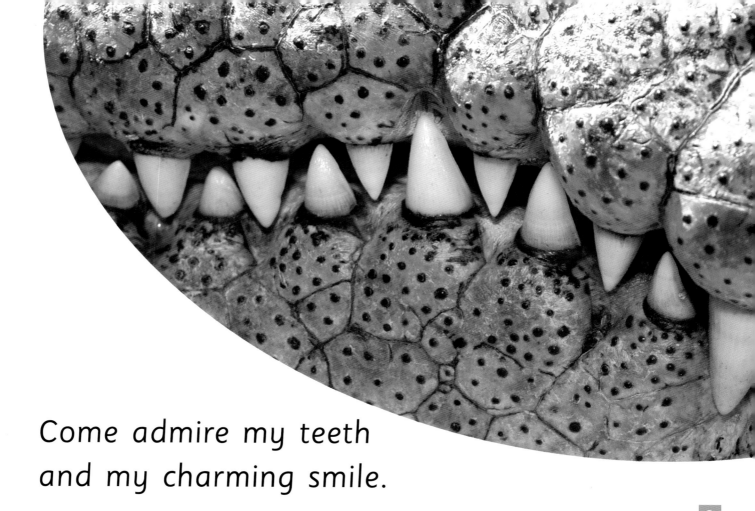

Come admire my teeth
and my charming smile.

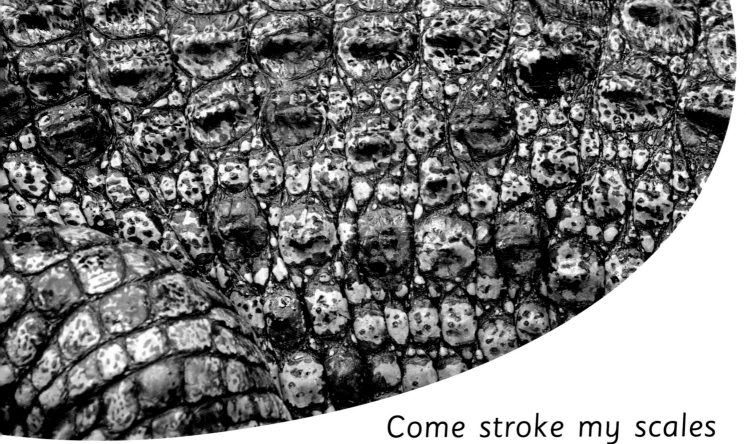

Come stroke my scales
that run down my back.

They keep my flesh safe
when I'm under attack.

Come snooze in the sun,
right here, beside me.

I look fast asleep—don't you agree?

Come watch me leap
from dark waters below.

Now you can see me...

but where did I go?

Come dive underwater
and you will see

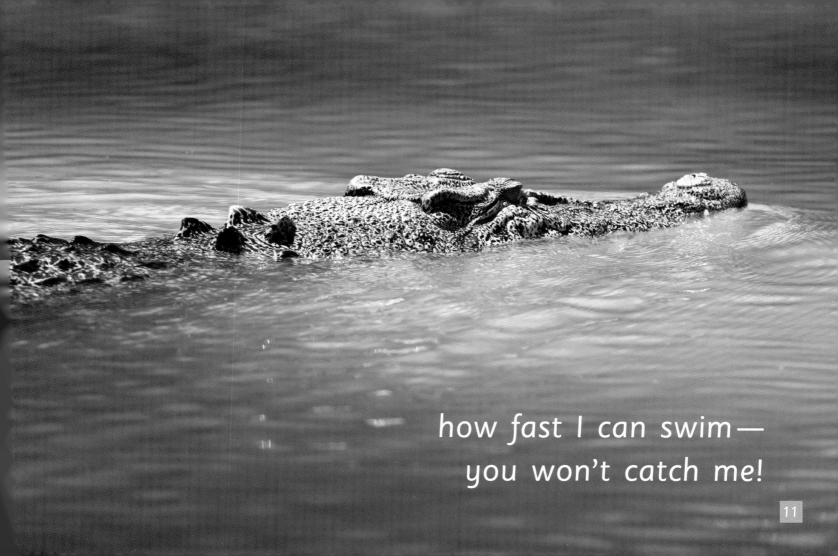

how fast I can swim—
you won't catch me!

Come watch me eat,
as I tear at my prey.

Are you sure I can't convince you to stay?

Come for a race,
up here on the sand.

I look so slow,
when I'm on the land.

Come meet my family,
they're a friendly bunch.

We'd love you to stay
for a bite of lunch!

Come see my eggs
that I've laid in the sand.

In three months they'll hatch,

if all goes to plan.

Come for a swim,
the water is fine.

DANGER
CROCODILES

NO
SWIMMING

20

Once you're in here with me,
we'll have a nice time.

Leaving so soon?
Did I scare you away?